Fart Wars

May the Farts Be With You

J.B. O'Neil

Published by JJ Fast Publishing LLC

Fart Wars

May the Farts Be With You

Table of Contents

For my son Joe, who loves to laugh about completely disgusting stuff like boogers, farts, Dutch ovens, wet willies, skid marks, ETC...Enjoy!

FREE BONUS – Fart Wars Audiobook

Hey gang…If you'd like to listen to the hilarious audiobook version of Fart Wars while you follow along with this book, you can download it for free for a limited time by going online and copying this link:

 http://funnyfarts.net/fartwars/

Enjoy!

Long Ago in a Galaxy Fart Fart Away...

I walked out of my house to check on the fart silos. They looked sort of like Igloos made of mud. It was so hot today...well, I mean everyday. There are two suns on my planet and it turns out with two suns, you get twice the heat, and a pretty nice tan if I do say so myself. I walked over to the silos to find that they were overflowing with farts. It was a good fart harvest this year.

"Milo! Milo Skyfarter!" That was my uncle calling me. I guess it was dinnertime. I walked back into my house and sat down to a big tall glass of blue milk.

Another Year Fart-Harvesting

"Milo, I have some bad news." My uncle said. He poured me another glass of blue milk. "You're going to have to spend another season here on the fart farm. There are just too many farts this year. I think it's all the blue milk."

I farted in anger. It was the milk.

"But I wanted to go to The Fart Academy this year. You said you'd let me go!" The saddest fart I ever farted leaked out. It sounded like my butt was crying.

"I'm so sorry Milo, but we need your help. You can go buy some robots to help us out with the workload though. That might let you go next year. There are just so many farts that we need to harvest."

I farted onto my feet and walked out. I was so mad at my uncle for not letting me go. My dream was to go to The Fart Academy with all of my friends. Well, maybe the new robots we were buying for the fart farm could help out enough that maybe I could go next year. It looked like I was never going to go on an adventure.

Out to Buy Some Robots

I woke up the next day to the sweet sweet smells of farts. The heat on my planet made the smell so much worse. I walked over to the robots shop, Bob's Bots, and started looking.

A bunch of the employees came up to me to help me pick one out. They were all short green men with gigantic heads. I found a robot that looked like a garbage can on wheels. Perfect. Garbage cans can hold a surprising amount of farts. I think that's why they smell so bad.

I knocked on its head to check it out and a hologram shot out of it. It was of a woman leaning over and she said "Help us Obi Fart-Nobi, you're our only hope." That was strange. I knew an old Ben Fart-Nobi. He was the crazy old man who lived alone in the mountains. What a strange little robot this was. Just as I was about to buy it, another robot came shuffling up to me. It was shiny and green and sort of looked like a person. It opened its mouth to say something, but farted instead. It sounded like static and smelled like gasoline. It made my eyes water. It came out black and looked like car exhaust.

Robots Fart Too

I told the green robot that I could only afford to buy one robot and that I was sorry but I was going to have to leave him behind. The green robot sighed and started to turn around, but a green alien man came running up to me waving his hands. He insisted that I take the green one. I didn't have to pay, they just wanted to get rid of it. He told me that the robot wouldn't stop farting and they couldn't take it anymore. All of their food started tasting like gasoline and they were starting to get hungry.

They wanted to give me a robot that farted all the time? Best thing ever! Who didn't want a farting robot? I agreed to take the robot off of their hands, out of good will, and made my way back to my house.

As I was beginning to think that this was actually going to be a good day, I saw a giant fart cloud coming from my house and fear went through my heart.

Ben Fart-Nobi

I ran as fast as I could to my house. There was so much gas. Green stinky gas. When I got there I saw my aunt and uncle lying on the ground, dazed from the terrible farts. I shook them to try to wake them up. "Uncle! Uncle, wake up! Please don't be dead!"

"Oh...Milo, is that you?" my Uncle murmered.

"Uncle, why!? Why are you dead Uncle!? WHY!?"

"Milo...I'm not dead..."

"Yes you are Uncle...yes you are...and I'm so sad about it...I'm going to leave and get revenge on whoever did this to you!"

"Milo, seriously...I'm not dead," my Uncle said. "You're trying to have an adventure and get out of farming, but you can't do that. You need to help on the farm."

"I'm going to find Old Man Fart-Nobi, he'll help me now that I'm all alone in the world!" I cried.

"Milo! Milo, dangit!" My uncle coughed out, but it was too late. I knew he was dead, even as he lay there and told me otherwise. Even if he wasn't dead, this was the best chance I could have to get off this planet and have an adventure. What was I supposed to do, stay behind and help?

I ran and got my robots and threw them into the back of my speeder. Then I jumped in the front and attached my fart nozzle so that I could power it and farted my way to the mountains. My farts were what powered the speeder and we went rocketing across the desert towards the mountains leaving a giant green trail behind us.

The Man in the Mountains

We pulled up at the foot of the mountains. Fart powered speeders can't move over mountains. We all got out. This was a little bit dangerous because these mountains were where the Fartskin Raiders lived. They were a vicious people whose skin was actually made of farts. Some people said that there was nothing worse than a Fartskin Raider. They were merciless farters who would fart in the face of anybody, no matter how helpless. Their skin was green and a little bit see through.

It was made of farts, after all.

We all started to slowly walk through the mountains, keeping a watchful eye out for Fartskin Raiders. I heard a rock fall behind me and I turned around to see a face full of Fartskin Raider butt! They had ambushed me! He farted straight into my face. It smelled so bad that my vision blurred and everything went hazy. I passed out. When I woke up, I was in a house with an old man leaning over me.

Obi Fart-Nobi, Master of the Farts

"Hello young Fartwalker." Said the old man. "I am Ben Fart-Nobi." I sat up and thanked him for saving me. I rubbed my face and moved over to the garbage can robot. I slammed it on the head and the hologram popped out.

It said, "I am Princess Lena Fartgana. The empire has taken me hostage and they plan to destroy the rebel alliance. Please help us Obi Fart-Nobi, you're our only hope."

Fart-Nobi thought to himself for a second, then looked up at me and said, "I haven't heard that name in a long long time. I haven't heard that name since I was a Fart Knight. We fought for good and for farts before the empire took over."

I looked at him, confused. "The Farts are what keep us all together, bind all living things. The Farts is a great force that can be used by the Fart Knights. It can also be used for the forces of evil. It may be that the empire is using the Farts as well."

Getting Some Helping Hands

Fart-Nobi looked at me and said, "It looks like we're going to need a ship to go save the princess. Looks like we'll need some help and I think I know where to find it."

"Oh man, this sounds serious. And important! Are we going on an adventure?" I asked.

"Well...yes Milo, I suppose we are. Do you need to get permission to come with me, perhaps from your surrogate family?"

I looked Obi Fart-Nobi straight in the eye, my jaw firmly set and my body trembling with righteous fury, infinite sadness, and terrible resolve. "My Uncle and Aunt were killed by farts. I want to find the people responsible! I have no home to return to."

"That's terrible," Fart-Nobi said. "I'm so sorry for you young Fartwalker. You will come with me, and I will train you in the ways of the Fart Knight."

We all got up and jumped back into my speeder and let loose the fart-powered engine, heading for the city. As we sped through the desert we passed my old house, where I could swear I could hear the ghostly calling of my Aunt and Uncle, asking me where I was going and telling me to check the fart silos. I will miss them so much....

In the city we stopped at the local cantina. "Um, Fart-Nobi? You sure we want to go in here?" I said.

"It looks like a box of farts on the outside, but it smells worse inside. I think this is where we'll find our pilot." Obi Fart-Nobi replied.

I didn't like the look of this place, and telling by the smell forming around me, it seemed like my butt didn't like it too much either. That was one scared fart. We walked in. Fart-Nobi told me to go hang out at the bar while he did some negotiating and walked off to a table. I walked over to the bar and ordered some blue milk. Then, two men approached me and they did not

26

seem all too friendly. One of them had a walrus face and was making crazy walrus noises at me and the other had doctor's scrubs on.

Not Quite Making Friends

The walrus man grabbed me by the front of my shirt and started shaking me while he made walrus noises. He spat so much. Then he put me down and his friend said, "My friend doesn't like you very much."

I looked at him and said, "Yeah, I didn't think he did. We don't even know each other though, why would he not like me?"

The doctor looked at me and said, "I don't like you either! I'm wanted in over twelve systems you know." He looked really impressed with himself.

Then, from a dark corner, there was this series of machine gun style farts. There were about fifty farts in about a second. Then a crown of people started running from where the farts came from with Fart-Nobi in the lead yelling "Run run run!" So I ran with him.

When we got to the door he stopped and let out the tiniest of tiny squeeker farts that turned into such a thick cloud that nobody could even walk through it.

"Where are we going!?" I yelled as we sprinted out of the cantina.

"I got us a pilot, co-pilot, and even a ship for them to pilot! Follow me," Obi Fart-Nobi said.

A Hop Skip and a Jump Through Space

We all ran as fast as we could onto a spaceship and not a moment too soon because a small army of Storm Farters were bent over and shooting some flaming hot farts at us. We could see the heat lines coming off of them.

We flew away and all sat down. One of the new guys was in a vest and the other looked like a giant bear, or a carpet. The one in the vest said his name was Hiney Solo and that his furry friend was Chewbuttka.

"I only took this job because I owe Jabba the Butt some farts and he's sending the bounty hunter Bobba Fart after me. That is a mean guy and when you owe him as many farts as I do, you learn to avoid him," said Hiney.

We all jumped into hyperspace leaving a nebula of farts behind us, but when we came out we saw something that should not have been there.

A Full Moon

"It looks like a small moon, but I don't remember there being any moon here." Said Hiney Solo.

"That's no moon," said Fart-Nobi, "We're being MOONED!"

There was a giant metal butt floating in space with the words "Galactic Farter, Property of the Empire" written just above the crack. The whole thing started rumbling before the biggest fart I had ever seen came out. It was green and in a perfectly straight line. It flew into a nearby planet and covered it in gas. The gas stayed around the entire planet. Those poor people had to smell that forever.

"We need to get out of here." Hiney said, but it was already too late. Our ship was moving straight for the Galactic Farter.

"They must have us caught in a tractor beam. We can't get out. It's too strong!" Hiney screamed.

The Belly of the Beast

We all hid in secret compartments as our ship got sucked into the Galactic Farter. When we finally landed I could hear a group of Storm Farters get on board, search the ship and leave without finding anything. When they were all gone we all stopped hiding and we snuck onto the Galactic Farter.

We split up so that we could get off this ship. Fart-Nobi went to find a way to shut down the tractor beam while Solo and Chewbuttka came with me to find and rescue the princess. We all headed to the control room to try and figure out where they were keeping the princess and save her.

Knockout Gas

When we got there, there were already two guards there.

"What do we do?" I asked.

"I think I know what to do." Answered Hiney. He walked up to them and farted in their faces.

"Don't worry," he said, "it was just knockout gas." We got on the computers and found out that they were keeping the princess on the jail level.

"Well, I guess that makes sense." I said. "But how do we get there?"

"I think I know!" said Hiney. "We can pretend that Chewbuttka is a prisoner and take him down there. All we need to do is to wear their uniforms and go."

That sounded like a good plan to me, so we took their uniforms and started going down. While we were doing that, Fart-Nobi was sneaking around trying to find his way to the tractor beam controls.

Not-so-Smooth Moves

We all walked into the jail, and before the guards could even look up, we bent over and unleashed a fart storm to knock them all out.

"PJ Farts, do you copy? PJ Farts, respond!" said a voice through the radio.

"We may not have thought this through." I said.

"It's fine, I'll handle this," said Hiney. He picked up the radio.

"Ah, copy roger copy. This is PJ Farts. There was a, um, a gas leak, but uh, we're fine. We're fine, we're all fine here. How are you?"

There was silence for a moment, but then the radio said, "We're sending down more guards. Something doesn't smell right here."

"That could have gone better." I said. The door opened and a ton more guards came in. They didn't even ask us who we were before they all let loose butt rockets and filled the whole room with gas.

Prison Break

We all ran down the hallway to where the prisoners were kept, farting back at the guards who were attacking us. I opened the cell that the princess was being held in and said, "We're here to save you."

"Looks like this isn't going well," said Lena. Her hair looked like a cinnamon role sitting on the top of her head.

I kept farting back as fast as I could, but then my butt overheated, letting loose a giant flare. I waved my hand over it to help it cool off; it also helped with the smell.

We were all farting back and forth and it started to look grim, but then Lena farted a whole in the ground. Her butt was still fresh and full of farts. She jumped through it and we all followed. It looked like we were home free until we realized where we landed: right in the middle of the main meeting room.

May the Farts be With You

We looked around, still ready to keep farting and we saw Obi Fart-Nobi fighting the greatest evil in the known universe, Dark Varter. They we both holding Fart-Sabers and fighting.

Obi Fart-Nobi looked over at me and said, "Use the Farts Milo. Use the Farts. May the Farts be with you." Then his Fart-Saber disappeared and Dark Varter struck him down. He disappeared completely in a cloud of gas. All that was left of Obi Fart-Nobi was a pile of terrible smelling clothes. "No!" I yelled.

The Melting Point

I was so mad, I started farting as fast and hot as I could. "Like a machine gun" is too slow to describe these farts. They were so hot, that eggs-pepper-and-Tabasco-sauce farts looked cold in comparison. I farted furiously, trying to hit anyone I could, and whatever my farts hit instantly melted. I could smell the anger in the farts. They came out pure red.

The Stormfarters all started farting back at me while Dark Varter walked towards us. I stood my ground and kept farting and farting. It was all that I could do.

"C'mon kid! We need to get out of here!" said Hiney as he grabbed me and pulled me onto the ship. We all got on board and we flew out of there as fast as we could.

Lena told us where the rebel base was and we set a course to there. I knew that we needed to get there as soon as we could so that we could take down the empire once and for all.

A Hole in the Plan

At the rebel base we all got together to try to figure out how to take down the Galactic Farter. We all got together in a large room with a giant hologram of the Galactic Farter floating in the middle. As we looked at it, I saw something amazing. There was a small hole on the surface that went all the way down to the core of the space station.

"I think that if we hit this hole with Fartton Torpedoes we can take down the whole ship." I said. There was an angry outburst from a bunch of the other pilots. They all thought that shot was impossible.

"I used to bulls-eye stink rats at eighty yards. This should be no problem." A bunch of them rolled their eyes, but I knew that this plan was the only chance that we had with our smaller numbers and weaker fart power.

Hiney So-Long!

We all started getting our piloting outfits on and getting in our ships when I saw Hiney Solo packing up his stuff.

"Why aren't you getting ready?" I asked. Hiney and Chewbuttka turned at looked at me and said,

"We're leaving. This fight isn't our fight. We're going to be long gone before this things breaks out."

I was shocked. I thought he was a hero! But he was acting like a coward.

"Why? Why won't you help us?" I asked.

He sighed. "I already got enough farts to pay back Jabba the Butt, so I'm leaving. I'm not going to risk our lives." I was so disappointed in him.

"Fine." I said, and stomped away to my ship.

Fight Farter with Farter

We all launched our ships and started our attack on the Galactic Farter. As we flew out in formation I said "Red Leader, checking in." I was answered with all of the other squadron leaders checking in. It looked like we were all ready to start the attack. We dove in at the Galactic Farter and as we got closer we saw thousands of butts sticking out of it pointing at us. They all started farting up at us.

"Weapons hot!" I called out and I started dodging farts as I flew it. Those we some terrible farts too.

If I got hit by one there was no way that I could keep fighting. I started farting back at them and picked up the speed.

A Fart and a Miss

We got to the trenches that lead to the hole we
needed to hit. Tie-Farters flew in behind us and
started farting. These farts smelled even worse
than the ones on the ship. Even as we dodged, a
few of us got hit and had to leave. There were so
many farts being fired at us that it was getting
harder and harder to dodge them all. Another
pilot fired the Fartton Torpedoes at the hole and
it looked like they hit, but nothing happened. It
seemed we weren't done yet...

Th-th-th-th-That's All Folks!

We flew up and out of the trenches so that we could get back up in our formation and get ready for our second attack. We flew back in, but this time it was much worse because Dark Varter himself was on our tail. He flew behind one of the pilots named Porkins.

"Porkins, he's right behind you! Pull up!" I yelled.

He wouldn't though. He did his best to dodge and he kept his eyes locked on his goal.

"Stay on target," he said.

"Pull up!" I yelled again.

"Stay on target."

Dark Varter fired his worst fart yet.

"Stay on target!"

"Porkins, no!" I cried, but it was too late. He was enveloped in a fart so foul that I knew he could not have survived. "PORKINS!"

But there was no time for grief. Dark Varter started to close the distance between us, lining me up in his targets, ready to take me down.

Use The Farts Milo

Just as he was about to fart and take me out, a familiar ship came flying out of space and smashed into Dark Varter. "

Yeehaw!" I heard through my radio.

"Hiney? Is that you?" I asked.

"You didn't think I was really going to let you take all the credit did you? Now let's go save the galaxy!"

"Thanks Hiney! I knew you'd come through." I turned on my targeting computer and flew in to finish this fight. Now, there was nothing between me and shooting some farts down that hole.

I was just about to take the shot when I heard a voice say, "Use the Farts Milo. Use the Farts." It was the voice of Obi Fart-Nobi.

"Is that you?" I asked.

"Yes Milo. Now use the Farts already. Jeeze, you take forever." I turned off my targeting computer and got in tune with the Farts. I felt the Farts. I *was* the Farts.

You Should Buy a New Butt, This One Has a Crack In It

"Hey buddy, is everything okay? You turned off your targeting computer." Said Hiney.

"Yeah," I said, "everything is going to be just fine."

I squinted my eyes and took a deep breath, then I fired my Fartton Torpedoes. It was the tensest moment of my life as I saw those farts fly to the hole. Then they hit and went in. I could immediately hear the Fartton Torpedoes moving through the Galactic Farter, growing as it went. Farts turning into farts and growing into a fart bigger than anyone had ever seen. The farts got to the fart core and that's when it happened. The fart had gotten so big and stinky that gas started shooting out through all of the cracks with such force, that the big crack in the middle started splitting open. The whole Galactic Farter broke in half from the crack cracking.

It was over. We had won.

"Let's go home guys. Our work here is done." I said, then turned my ship around and flew back to base.

Alls Well That Farts Well

When I got back, I was greeted by a group of cheering people who carried me out of my ship. I crowd surfed all the way to the throne room where Princess Lena was waiting for us. They dropped me onto my feet next to Hiney Solo and Chewbuttka. They both looked at me and smiled.

"Nice job kid." Said Hiney, elbowing me in the ribs.

"Thanks," I replied. Music started playing and we all started to walk forward towards Princess Lena who was waiting for us, holding medals.

I walked up to her.

"Thank you for everything you've done for us Milo Skyfarter. You are a true hero," she announced to the crowd. She lifted up the medal and as she was putting it over my head, a very loud, staticky fart rang out throughout the throne room. Everybody looked over and saw the green robot. I wanted to say something, but the fart smelled so bad that I couldn't even talk. My eyes were watering so badly seeing was getting hard.

I finally choked out, "Maybe we should have brought him on the attack. We wouldn't even need to aim him!" Everybody laughed, then coughed, and then removed the robot from the room.

MORE FUNNY FARTS...

If you laughed really hard at Fart Wars, I know you'll love these other stinky bestselling books by J.B. O'Neil (for kids of *all* ages!)

http://jjsnip.com/fart-book

And...

http://jjsnip.com/booger-fart-books

Silent but Deadly...As a Ninja Should Be!

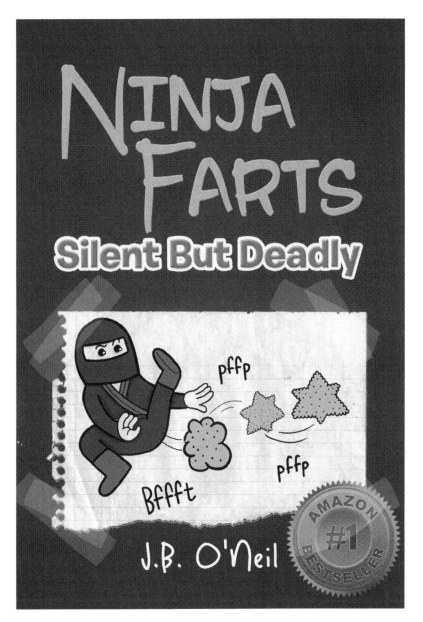

http://jjsnip.com/ninja-farts-book

Did you know cavemen farted?

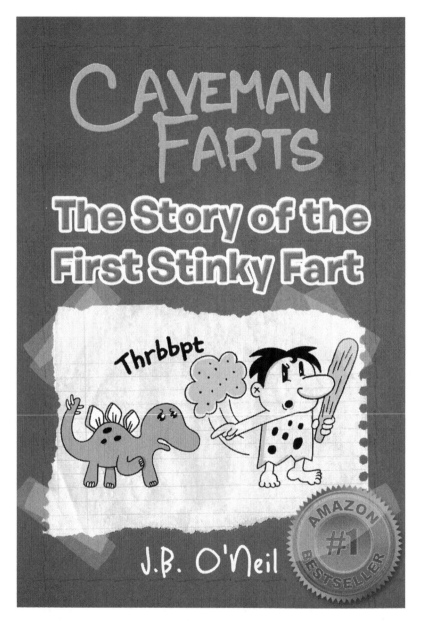

http://jjsnip.com/caveman-farts

Think twice before you blame the dog!

http://jjsnip.com/dog-farts

And check out my new series, the

Family Avengers!

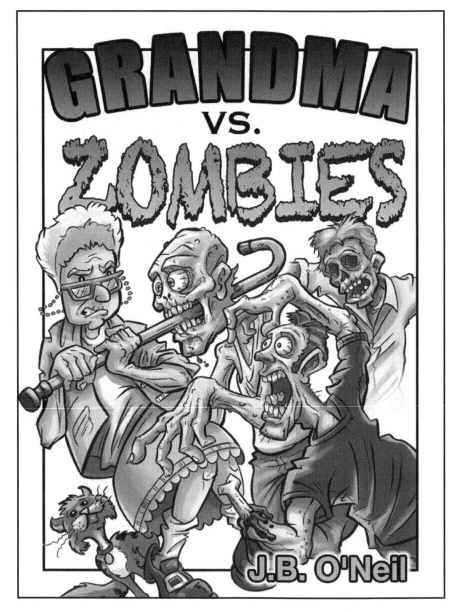

http://jjsnip.com/gvz